The ratchaphruek, or golden shower, is the Thai national flower.

Spirit houses are small shrines meant to provide shelter for spirits, often with offerings of food and drink.

Mudmee is a type of patterned fabric weaving, usually with silk, that dates back three thousand years.

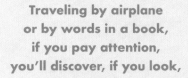

Traveling by airplane
or by words in a book,
if you pay attention,
you'll discover, if you look,

what makes up a culture,
the places and things
that make a place special,
that make a place sing.

On each page that follows,
a small surprise you will find.
To learn about Thailand,
use your eyes and your mind.

The Siamese fireback, the Thai national bird, is a pheasant with red legs and gray-blue feathers.

A sala is a traditional Thai open pavilion, a nice shady spot on a hot day.

A phin is a lute with three metal strings.

Bala Kids
An imprint of Shambhala Publications, Inc.
2129 13th Street
Boulder, Colorado 80302
www.shambhala.com

Cover art: Marisa Aragón Ware
Design: Kara Plikaitis

9 8 7 6 5 4 3 2 1

First Edition
Printed in China

♾ This edition is printed on acid-free paper that meets the American National Standards Institute Z39.48 Standard.
♲ Shambhala makes every effort to print on postconsumer recycled paper. For more information please visit www.shambhala.com.
Bala Kids is distributed worldwide by Penguin Random House, Inc., and its subsidiaries.

Library of Congress Cataloging-in-Publication Data
Names: Aragón Ware, Marisa, author, illustrator.
Title: Bodhi sees the world: Thailand / Marisa Aragón Ware.
Description: First edition. | Boulder, Colorado: Bala Kids, an imprint of Shambhala Publications, Inc., [2021] | Audience: Ages 3–6. | Audience: Grades K–1.
Identifiers: LCCN 2020053486 | ISBN 9781611808261 (hardback)
Subjects: CYAC: Voyages and travels—Fiction. | Bangkok (Thailand)—Fiction. | Thailand—Fiction.
Classification: LCC PZ7.1.A71982 Bod 2021 | DDC [E]—dc23
LC record available at https://lccn.loc.gov/2020053486

BODHI SEES the WORLD

THAILAND

Marisa Aragón Ware

bala kids

High above the Andaman Sea, over the clouds in the clear, calm air, Bodhi is on her way to Thailand.

When the plane touches down, the sights and sounds of Bangkok blossom all around.

The city is a symphony of noise! Horns beep, engines roar . . .

. . . and a language Bodhi doesn't understand swirls around her like a river of words.

Aroi mak mak!

อร่อยมากๆ

Khop khun ka!

ขอบคุณค่ะ

And suddenly, a long, long way from home,
Bodhi feels like she doesn't quite belong.

"Pi nigh krub?" the tuk-tuk driver calls as Bodhi and her mom climb aboard.

They zip and zoom through the bustling city streets. The stinky smell of traffic blends with the sweet scent of fruit and incense, making Bodhi's head spin. She shuts her eyes tight and wishes she could go home.

"Bodhi, look!" says her mom as the tuk-tuk slows, and she sees beautiful golden spires and temple guardians sparkling in the sun.

Inside the temple, the world is quiet. Bodhi
sits still, listening to the silence.

She watches as nuns make offerings to the Emerald Buddha.

One by one, they lay a garland of yellow marigolds at the base of the statue with a gentle bow.

The nuns walk so calmly that all the meditating people can feel their peace.

Bodhi leaves the temple full of wonder. Now with a quiet mind, she notices that things are not so different here in Bangkok.

The sun and the clouds are the same.
The grass is green and the trees are tall.

Kids laugh and play, just like her
friends back home do, and a smile
is the same in any language.

Suddenly curious to explore, Bodhi boards
a boat to the famous floating market.

Boats with piles of coconuts, bananas, and dragon fruits bustle along the crowded river.

Bodhi's mom buys her green curry, yellow mango, and sticky white rice.

The flavors mix in her mouth, a parade of honey sweet and hot, fiery spice. It's like nothing she's ever tasted—and she likes it!

A line of monks walk through the market with empty bowls in their hands. They rely on the generosity of people to feed them.

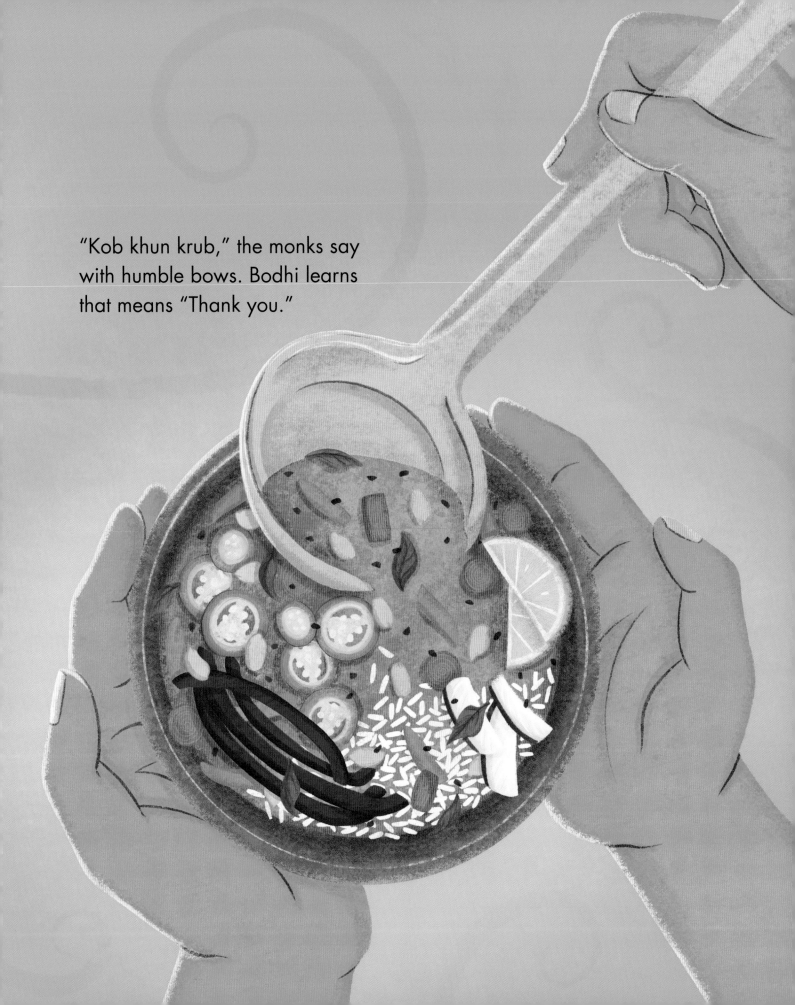

"Kob khun krub," the monks say with humble bows. Bodhi learns that means "Thank you."

She walks on through the market to the edge of the river. Something sparkles deep inside a dark barrel, a flicker of silver catching the sun.

Inside, Bodhi sees tiny fish flash and whirl in the crowded water. Her heart stirs, like it's waking up from a long nap.

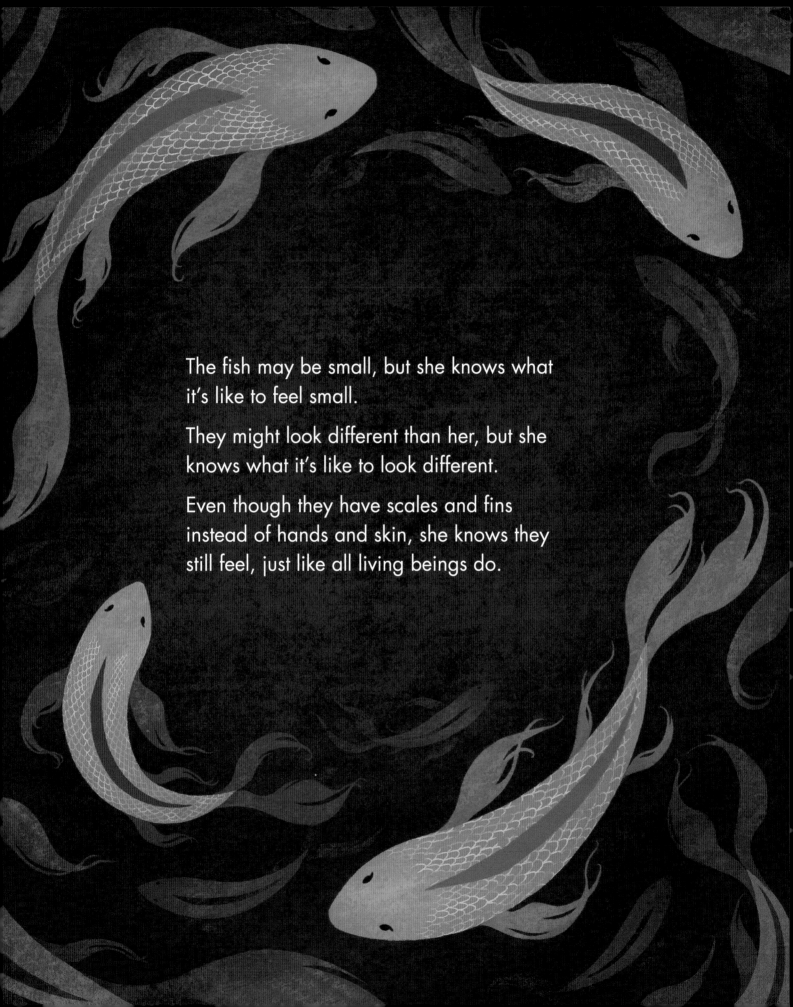

The fish may be small, but she knows what it's like to feel small.

They might look different than her, but she knows what it's like to look different.

Even though they have scales and fins instead of hands and skin, she knows they still feel, just like all living beings do.

An old woman notices Bodhi, and with a warm smile, she pays the man selling the fish one hundred baht. He scoops them into two little bags and hands one to Bodhi.

For a moment, the old woman stands still, eyes closed. Then, quick as a flap of a bird's wing, she pours the fish back into the river, their home.

Bodhi knows just what to do. She stands still and closes her eyes. She takes a deep breath.

Then she sets the fish free.
Bodhi's heart blooms.

As the sun goes down, the people of Bangkok gather to celebrate Loi Krathong, a holiday of giving thanks. They light lanterns and float shining baskets of flowers down the river.

A little girl helps Bodhi make a raft out of a
banana leaf, and together they light a candle.

She sets the raft in the river, and suddenly, a long, long way from home . . .

Bodhi feels like she is right where she belongs.

About Bangkok

Bangkok is the capital city of Thailand. There are 5.67 million people living there—more than any other city in Thailand.

The weather in Thailand can be quite hot! It has a tropical climate with three seasons: hot, rainy, and cool. During the rainy season, there are big rainstorms called monsoons.

A tuk-tuk is just like a taxi, but it has only three wheels—one in the front and two in the back. They are named after the sound they make when they drive by. *Pi nigh krub* means "Where are you going?"

 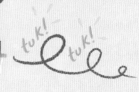

Loi Krathong is an annual festival celebrated on a full moon in late fall in the Western calendar. Participants make decorated baskets called *krathong* from leaves that float on the river. People often put beautiful flowers, incense, coins, or small bits of food on their krathong as an offering to the river spirits.

The Grand Palace, which began construction in 1782, is one of the most popular tourist attractions and is located at the heart of Bangkok. The king and his court used to live there. Today it is still used for royal ceremonies.

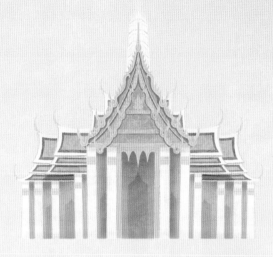

The Emerald Buddha is a sacred statue made of green jasper and gold that is housed in a temple called Wat Phra Kaew. It is estimated to be at least six hundred years old.

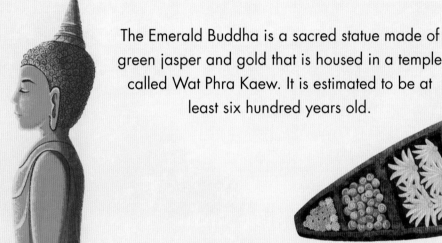

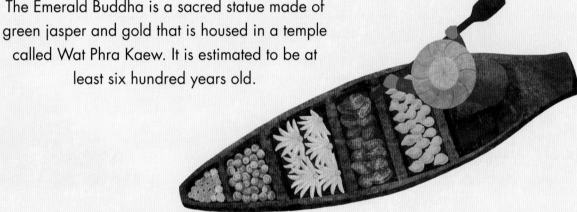

Bangkok has numerous floating markets where people buy and sell fruits, vegetables, spices, and other items on boats and by the sides of the river. Live fish and other animals are often sold there, and it is a Buddhist practice to buy these living creatures and then set them free in their natural environment, saving lives and generating good karma.

In Thailand, the money is called baht. The colorful paper banknotes show pictures of King Rama IX, who lived from 1927–2016. His son, Rama X, became the next king.

The Chao Phraya River runs through Bangkok all the way to the Gulf of Thailand. Before modern roads were built, the river was the main method of transportation.

Author's Note

Once upon a time there was a little girl named Marisa who often traveled the world with her parents. That little girl grew up to be me, and now that I'm grown-up I want to share the magic of traveling to new places with you. I named the character in this book Bodhi, which means *awake* or *completely open*, because I think that describes the feeling that traveling can create. When we are in a new place, we might feel a sense of wonder or pay more attention to the details of life than when we are in our familiar surroundings.

I've always been curious about how people in other parts of the world live, being the product of two different cultures myself. Growing up, I heard my mom and her family speaking Spanish interchangeably with English. I also saw how my father would make an effort to learn as much of the language of whatever country we were traveling in as he could. All these experiences have been distilled into the character of Bodhi, who happens to have an uncanny resemblance to a six-year-old me. Bodhi's curiosity and mindfulness, as well as her open-hearted approach to new experiences, can teach us how we can be kinder and more present in our daily lives. Enjoy the journey!

In Thailand, how do you say...

Hello
(if you are a girl)

Sawadee ka
สวัสดีค่ะ

Hello
(if you are a boy)

Sawadee krub
สวัสดีครับ

Goodbye

La kon
ลาก่อน

Yes

Chai
ใช่

No

Mai
ไม่

Friend

Phuuan
เพื่อน